MY FIRST

Sticker
Copy and Color

make
believe
ideas

Have fun using stickers and color to finish the pictures!

1 Find the sticker sheets at the back of the book. Look for the stickers for the page you are working on. Place them on the picture where you see this grid pattern:

2 Look at the pictures. Sometimes half an image is already colored. Color the other half of the image the same colors. Then finish coloring the rest of the page to complete your picture.

3 Sometimes there are two images of the same thing in a picture – one is already colored and the other one is for you to color. You can copy the colors already on the page or, if you prefer, use other colors.

4 There are some extra stickers at the back of the book. You can use these in the book or wherever you want.

Have fun!

Handsome Ted

Add the stickers, and then finish coloring the other half of the picture.

Fluttering butterflies

5

Playful pup

Woof!
Woof!

Cool lighthouse

8

Double trouble

Add the stickers, and then color the big dinosaur the same colors as the little one.

High in
the sky

Cute cat

What is the cat wearing?

Digging dirt

Add the stickers. Then color the digger the same colors as the digger on the sticker.

Funky flowers

Buzz!
Buzz!

Lovely ladybugs

15

Jungle fun

Where do tigers live?

Alien travels

17

Tim and Tom

Zippy zebras

22

Race to the moon

23

Colorful clothes

Under the sea

Add the stickers. Then match the animal friends, and color them the same colors.

Can you find a sea star?

27

Happy homes

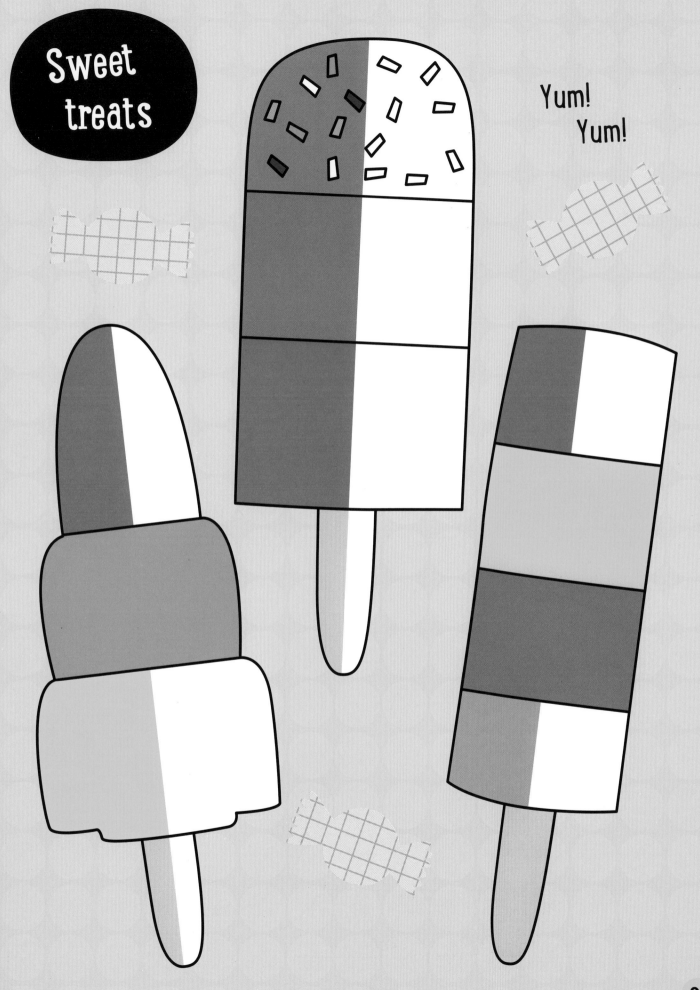

Sweet treats

Yum! Yum!

Dino dance

Let's dance together!

Puffed-up puffer fish

Oodles of owls

Hoot!
Hoot!

33

Campfire fun

36

Stickers for pages 4-5

Stickers for pages 6-7

Stickers for pages 10-11

Stickers for pages 8-9

Stickers for pages 12-13

Stickers for pages 14-15

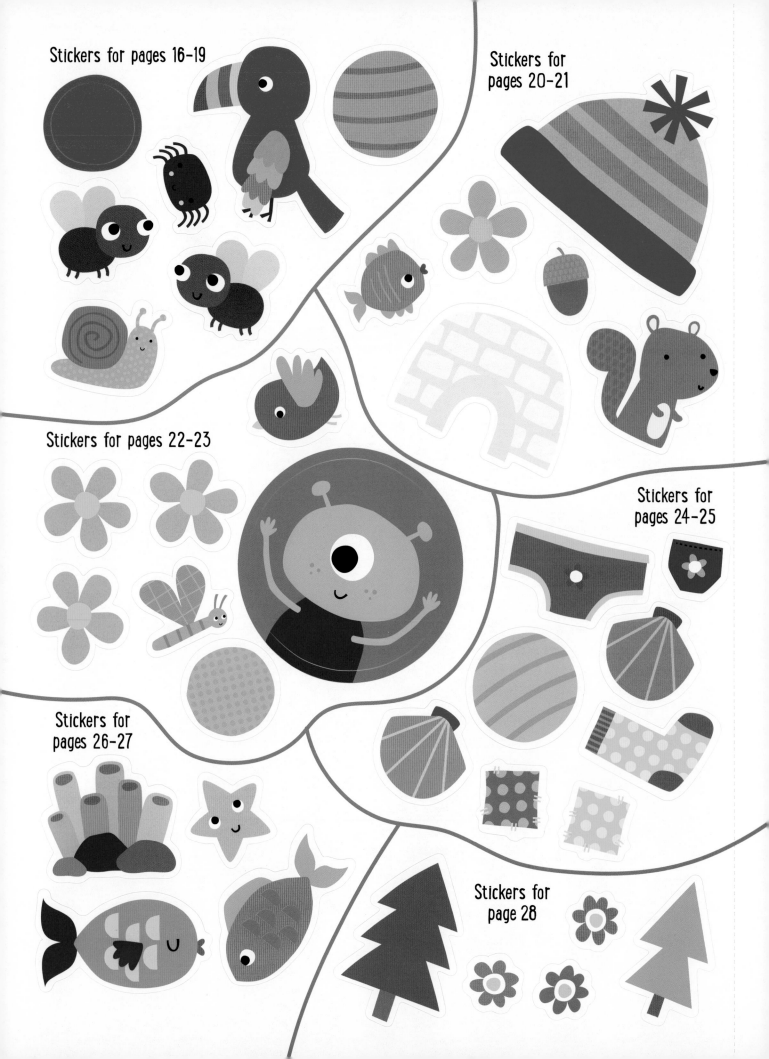

Stickers for pages 16-19

Stickers for pages 20-21

Stickers for pages 22-23

Stickers for pages 24-25

Stickers for pages 26-27

Stickers for page 28

Stickers for page 29

Stickers for pages 30-31

Stickers for pages 32-33

Stickers for pages 34-35

Stickers for pages 36-37

Stickers for pages 38-40

Extra stickers

Extra stickers

Extra stickers

Extra stickers

Extra stickers